The Enchanted Kingdom

Translated by Polly Lawson
First published in Italian as *Il Regno incantato*
© 1997 Edizione Arka, Milan
English version © 2000 by Floris Books, 15 Harrison Gardens, Edinburgh
British Library CIP Data available
ISBN 0-86315-333-X
Printed in Italy

The Enchanted Kingdom

Guido Visconti
Illustrated by Maria Battaglia

Floris Books

A king once ruled over a sun-scorched land where there were no trees, no birds, no flowers. The entire kingdom was desert.

"What dark magic made the beauty of nature vanish from my kingdom?" the king wondered.

"There is no such thing as magic," explained his first minister, "Years ago, the trees were cut down to build castles and palaces. Then it rained less and less, and the birds and flowers disappeared too. Finally the wind turned the gardens into sand."

One day, a merchant arrived, selling fabrics and tapestries woven with gold and silver.

"Which one would you like?" the King asked his daughter.

"The one with the birds and the trees," she cried. "It's beautiful!"

"In my country," the merchant said, "we have so many trees, bright with leaves and flowers and fruit. Birds sing in their branches. Children play in their shade."

The king sighed unhappily.

That night, the little princess could not stop thinking about the birds in the trees. She kept hearing her father's unhappy sighs.

Suddenly, she had an idea.

The next morning, she left the castle, and ran to one of the towers that dominated the city. She climbed all the way to the top.

At the very top there lived the best painter in the kingdom.

"Do you think you could paint me some birds?" she asked.

"What a wonderful idea," he said, and found his brushes straight away.

He went over to the wall and started painting many different birds.

The little princess clapped her hands with joy. Suddenly, there was a flutter of wings.

One by one, the birds flew away from the wall and out of the tower window.

Within moments the city was full of birdsong.

The people were amazed. The king looked out of his window.

"What magic is this?" he asked his first minister.

"There is no such thing as magic," he replied, shaking his head. "They are only migrating birds, and tomorrow they will be gone."

That evening the king sat in one of the castle towers, watching the stars. He heard the nightingales sing in the darkness, and stayed up all night listening to their song.

"My minister is right," he sighed sadly. "Tomorrow they will be gone."

The next day, the birds were still there. But they stopped singing and hid beneath the roofs to shelter from the sun.

The little princess ran back to the tower.

"The birds are not happy here," she told the painter. "It is too hot for them."

The painter went over to the wall and started to paint white fluffy balls.

"Now, come over here and blow hard," he said to her.

The little princess huffed and puffed. Slowly the white fluffy balls started to glide out of the window.

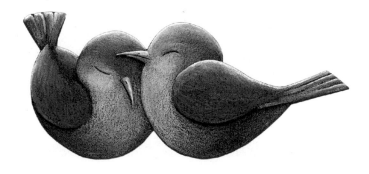

Cries of surprise were heard all over the kingdom.

"Look! Clouds are coming!"

"Impossible, they are only dust clouds from the desert," said the first minister.

Then cries of joy rang out.

"It's raining! It's really raining!"

It rained all day. The birds left their hiding places and started to sing once again.

The king looked up into the sky, his heart beginning to lift with hope.

Now the seeds which had been sleeping in the soil were awoken by the rain. The next morning the kingdom was full of plants and flowers of every colour.

The birds ate the berries and filled the air with song. The children played among the flowers, and discovered their wonderful smells.

"The clouds have already gone," said the first minister. "By tomorrow the plants will start to disappear."

The king did not want to listen, and went for a walk in the castle gardens. He smelt the sweet perfume of the roses, and marvelled at the beauty all around him.

"Surely some kind of magic has brought my kingdom back to life," he said to himself.

"It was your daughter!" said a voice behind him.

The King turned and there was the old painter.

"My daughter?" he asked.

"Yes, she asked me to paint the birds. Nature seen through the eyes of a child is a magical thing, and all the birds took flight."

"But your painting is also magical," said the King, "because it brought everything to life." And he was so happy that he hugged the old painter.

The days passed and the kingdom seemed more and more like a little paradise.

Children danced and played beneath the trees. The air was full of birdsong.

"My kingdom is very blessed," said the king.

"Now I believe," said the first minister,
"it is truly an enchanted kingdom."

"Yes," the king smiled, "for once you are
right. This is the work of a great magician
and his fairy helper!" And he laughed, and
kept his daughter's secret to himself.